BONKO ON THE TRAPEZE

Molly Burkett
and
Adrian Metcalfe

This book is dedicated to Tracey Charlotte

Bonko is a clown, and a very happy clown too. He is happy because he makes people laugh and Bonko likes seeing people laugh.

You might have seen Bonko when you have been to the circus. He is the little, fat clown, the one that always seems to do the wrong thing.

He is the clown who looks down the hosepipe to see where the water is, and it spurts all over his face. It is Bonko who tries to drive the old car round the ring, but he presses the wrong knobs and pulls the wrong handles. Instead of going forwards the car goes backwards, and when Bonko wants the car to stop, it goes very, very quickly and he cannot get out. Then when he presses another knob, the car blows up and there is Bonko, sitting on the seat but the wheels have fallen off and the engine is on fire. So then Tilly and Tally, the pierrots who work in the circus with Bonko, run and fetch buckets of water to put out the fire, but they throw too hard and the water goes all over Bonko. So Bonko gets some water and throws it at Tilly and Tally, and it finishes up by Tally tipping a whole bucketful over Bonko's head, bucket and all, and Bonko sits down in the middle of a puddle of water because he cannot see where he is going.

One day, there was a problem at the circus. The trapeze man had toothache. It was really bad toothache. The problem was that his tooth began to hurt five minutes before his act was due to start.

"It's no good," he told Janet, his assistant, "I can't go on with this pain. I must go and find a dentist."

"What shall we do?" Janet asked. "You can't have a circus without a trapeze act."

"It's no good," said John, "I wouldn't be safe up there with a toothache like this. You'd better tell the ringmaster."

The ringmaster came out to see Janet and John.

"Well, we can't have a circus without a trapeze act," he said.

Janet said "I'm alright. I'll do the act on my own. I'll just need someone up on the platform with me to swing the trapeze to me when I shout. Anyone can do that."

That was when Bonko came out of the ring. He had just finished his act and he was very wet. He was looking forward to changing into his dry clothes, but the ringmaster did not give him a chance.

"Oh Bonko," his voice boomed, "I want your help. I want you to go and help Janet on the trapeze."

Now Bonko is a friendly fellow and he will

do anything to help anyone, well nearly anything. His idea of helping stopped a long way short of helping Janet on a trapeze. Bonko was very fond of his feet, but he liked to have them firmly on the ground. The thought of swinging backwards and forwards on a trapeze with his feet beneath him and all that empty space beneath them, made Bonko feel decidedly sick.

The ringmaster is a very tall, very stern man. He is in charge of the circus and all the circus folk are a little bit frightened of him. He is a thin man, and always wears a red jacket and black trousers with black leather boots and a black top hat. He has a long, thin moustache that is too long for his face and he always carries a whip which he cracks on the ground when he is angry.

Bonko was a little frightened of the ringmaster but was a lot more frightened of the trapeze. He started to explain this to the ringmaster, but Janet laughed and interrupted.

"Bonko, we don't want you to perform on the trapeze, all we want you to do is to stand on the platform and swing the trapeze to me when I shout. That's all."

That sounded more than enough to Bonko,

but he was so relieved to find that he did not have to swing on a trapeze, and turn himself into all sorts of shapes that he forgot to complain. Then he did not have time because the ringmaster was leading them both into the ring and a voice was announcing the great trapeze artistes Janet and John.

When the audience saw Janet and Bonko coming into the ring they started to laugh and clap. They all thought it was part of Bonko's act.

Now there are two platforms high above everyone's heads in the roof of the big top and there is a trapeze tied to the side of each platform. There are two long rope ladders, each leading to one of the platforms.

Janet went to the foot of one of the ladders and the ringmaster led Bonko to the bottom of the other.

Bonko took off his three foot long shoes that he wore in his act. It would be easier to climb the ladder in his socks. He was not going to leave his Bonko stick behind, oh dear no.

Then the band was playing some special music and Janet and Bonko were climbing the ladders, one rung at a time. Bonko felt decidedly ill by the time he reached the third. The trouble was that the rope ladder did not feel very safe. It twisted and turned every time Bonko moved, and Bonko's stomach twisted and turned too. He held onto the rope and moaned "I want to come down."

"Hurry up Bonko," the ringmaster ordered, "you're getting left behind. Whatever you do don't look down. DON'T LOOK DOWN."

So Bonko climbed higher and higher. He looked across at Janet. She was doing acrobatics on the rope ladder. The sight of her made Bonko feel ill. It was as much as he could do to lift one foot up and make it go up to the the next rung, but Janet was holding on with only her hands and swinging out to one side and then the other. She even turned

AJM.

upside-down. Then she held on to the ladder with one foot and stretched out like a star — that was not so clever.

"I can do that," Bonko thought, "well, I can do a bit of it." And he let go of the ladder with one hand and stretched out with one little short arm. Somehow it did not look like the shape Janet made and it did not feel very comfortable either. The audience liked it though. They laughed and cheered, so Bonko made another pattern with his left arm this time.

Then Bonko had reached the platform. He stood on it and shivered with fright. To start with, it had taken him five minutes to get on the platform and stand up. Everyone had thought he was acting, and had laughed and cheered. But Bonko was not acting. He was just plain frightened and he was even more frightened now he was on the platform. There was not anything secure to hold on to. The platform wobbled and Bonko wobbled. He wished he was back on the ground.

Then Janet started her act. She swung on her trapeze. She did somersaults on her trapeze. Then she hung on with one hand then one foot. Bonko could hardly bear to watch her. Then she shouted to Bonko, "When I shout 'Go!', swing that trapeze towards me."

Bonko did that and when the second trapeze was nearly touching her own, Janet let go of her trapeze and caught hold of the one Bonko had swung. For a second or two she had not been holding on to anything at all. She really had been flying through the air. Then she swung back to her own trapeze again and shouted to Bonko to catch his. If you remember, he had taken his Bonko stick with him and his Bonko stick is like any ordinary walking stick except that it has balloons on the end you generally put on the ground. Well, he reached out with the hook of his stick and drew the trapeze towards him. He did not mind doing that. He swung the trapeze when Janet shouted and pulled it back to the platform when she told him. It was so easy that he forgot thinking about where he was and of the dreadful journey he would have to make to get back down on to the ground again. I suppose he was getting a bit too confident altogether because he reached out with his Bonko stick to draw the trapeze in, and I do not know if his foot slipped, or he leaned out a bit too far, but suddenly he was swinging out over the heads of all those people, holding on to his Bonko stick and his

Bonko stick was hooked firmly over the trapeze. At first the trapeze and the Bonko stick and Bonko swung in a great arc once, twice, three times, then the swinging slowed down and stopped and there was Bonko hanging there, suspended beneath the Big Top. He suddenly felt very ill indeed.

"Help," he said, "help." But no one heard him. They all thought this was part of his act and the funniest thing they had ever seen — they laughed and shouted and cheered.

"Bonko," shouted Janet, "swing, move your legs and make yourself swing, I'll swing out and meet you and pull you back to the platform."

Bonko did move his legs up and down, just a little, but that did not make him swing, not even half an inch. He stayed just where he was.

"Bonko," Janet called, "let go and drop down. There's a safety net there. You can't hurt yourself. It's perfectly safe."

That was when Bonko looked down to see where the safety net was. He did not see the safety net, but he did see what a long way he was from the ground. No way was Bonko going to let go. He shook his head from side to side. He tried to say "Help," but no noise came out of his mouth when he opened it. Bonko was sure of one thing and that was that he was not going to let go of anything.

Tilly and Tally climbed up the rope ladders to the platforms in the air. They tried to make Bonko let go of his Bonko stick and land in the safety net.

"Look," Tilly and Tally told him, "look at us. We'll jump into the safety net and you'll see how easy it is."

So Tilly and Tally jumped into the safety net to show Bonko how safe it was, then they called for Bonko to jump too, but Bonko shook his head. He was going to stay just where he was.

Then the lady with the chimpanzees

climbed up the rope ladder and tried to persuade Bonko to let go and jump. Then the elephant man, and the dog trainer and the girls who ride the horses. Even the ringmaster himself climbed up the rope ladder to the platform. They all tried to persuade Bonko to let go and jump, and they all jumped into the safety net to show him how easy it was. The elephant man jumped, the dog trainer jumped, the girls who ride the horses jumped.

Even the ringmaster jumped, but Bonko did not jump. He stayed exactly where he was.

The audience laughed and laughed. They thought it was part of the act, but the circus folk were worried. However could they get Bonko down from the trapeze?

Then Long John arrived. Long John was Bonko's best friend and he was very long indeed, he was certainly the longest man that Bonko had ever seen.

Long John did not know that Bonko was on the trapeze. He had come to see his friend and when he saw him hanging on to the trapeze by his Bonko stick Long John's mouth fell open in surprise.

He went straight to his car and collected the longest stilts he had. He fastened them to his feet and stood up, but even then he was not tall enough to reach Bonko although his eyes were almost level with Bonko's feet.

"Now don't be frightened Bonko," Long John said, in his slow, deep voice. "You know

what we do when we feel unhappy, we sing a happy song and we clap our hands. Let's do that now."

Long John started to sing and then he clapped his hands. Bonko copied him. He sang and clapped his hands too. He could not clap and hold on to his Bonko stick at the same time, could he? Suddenly, Bonko was

falling down into the safety net and Tilly and Tally and all the little Tallys were there to help him get down to the ground. All the people were cheering. They thought it was the best circus act they had ever seen. The circus folk were happy. They were pleased that Bonko was safe and sound.

Bonko was the only one who was not smiling. He had not enjoyed the adventure at all.

"Do you know," he told Long John when they were back in his little round caravan, drinking cocoa and eating strawberry jam sandwiches and doughnuts, "I don't want to see another trapeze as long as I live."

But he did. Bonko worked in a circus so he saw Janet and John and the trapeze every time he went to work. After all, you cannot have a circus without a trapeze can you?